Gemstone Dragons

TOPAZ'S SPOOKY NIGHT

The Gemstone Dragons series

Gemstone Dragons

TOPAZ'S SPOOKY NIGHT

Samantha M. Clark

ILLUSTRATED BY
Hollie Hibbert

BLOOMSBURY
CHILDREN'S BOOKS
NEW YORK   LONDON   OXFORD   NEW DELHI   SYDNEY

BLOOMSBURY CHILDREN'S BOOKS
Bloomsbury Publishing Inc., part of Bloomsbury Publishing Plc
1385 Broadway, New York, NY 10018

BLOOMSBURY, BLOOMSBURY CHILDREN'S BOOKS, and the Diana logo
are trademarks of Bloomsbury Publishing Plc

First published in the United States of America in December 2022
by Bloomsbury Children's Books

Text copyright © 2022 by Samantha M. Clark
Illustrations copyright © 2022 by Hollie Hibbert, in the style of Janelle Anderson

Bloomsbury books may be purchased for business or promotional use.
For information on bulk purchases please contact Macmillan Corporate and
Premium Sales Department at specialmarkets@macmillan.com

Library of Congress Cataloging-in-Publication Data
Names: Clark, Samantha M., author. | Hibbert, Hollie, illustrator.
Title: Topaz's spooky night / by Samantha M. Clark ; illustrated by Hollie Hibbert.
Description: New York : Bloomsbury Children's Books, 2022. | Series: Gemstone dragons ;
book 3 | Audience: Ages 7–10 | Audience: Grades 2–3
Summary: Topaz hides her fear of the dark by using her power over light, but one day
she discovers her power is gone and she must find a way to face her fears to help
the other dragons when disaster strikes one moonless night.
Identifiers: LCCN 2022022253 (print) | LCCN 2022022254 (e-book)
ISBN 978-1-5476-1089-1 (paperback) • ISBN 978-1-5476-1090-7 (e-book)
Subjects: CYAC: Fantasy. | Dragons—Fiction. | Fear of the dark—Fiction. |
Self confidence—Fiction. | Magic—Fiction. | Friendship—Fiction. | LCGFT: Fantasy fiction.
Classification: LCC PZ7.1.C579 To 2022 (print) | LCC PZ7.1.C579 (e-book) | DDC [Fic]—dc23
LC record available at https://lccn.loc.gov/2022022253
LC e-book record available at https://lccn.loc.gov/2022022254

Book design by Jeanette Levy
Typeset by Westchester Publishing Services
Printed and bound in the U.S.A.
2 4 6 8 10 9 7 5 3 1

To find out more about our authors and books
visit www.bloomsbury.com and sign up for our newsletters.

For Sabrina,

who used to tell her own spooky stories

Gemstone Dragons

TOPAZ'S SPOOKY NIGHT

chapter one

A SPOOKY STORY

It was a beautiful clear night in Gemstone Valley with only a sliver of moon in the sky. The dragons were on top of Mineral Mountain enjoying a meteor shower. The dark night made the stars look extra bright, but it also made Topaz extra nervous.

Topaz didn't like the dark. When she couldn't see, she was afraid monsters were going to jump out at her.

She concentrated on the topaz gemstone on her chest, activating its power, and as her yellow-brown scales rippled, light glowed all around her. She felt much better.

"Why are you turning on your light out here, Topaz?" Emerald asked.

"I don't want anyone to trip on a rock," Topaz said, which was only a little true. She didn't want to admit the real reason.

"That's very nice of you," Ruby said. Topaz loved the way her best friend always defended her.

"Thank you, Ruby." Topaz gave her a small smile.

"It is nice, but then we can't see the stars," Emerald said. "You can turn it off now. We'll be all right."

"That reminds me of a joke." Aquamarine did a little skip. "Why did the monster eat Topaz? Because it wanted a light lunch! Get it? Because her power is light?" He bent over laughing, but the other dragons didn't find it funny, especially Topaz. She didn't want to think about being eaten by a monster.

Aquamarine gazed at the dragons' stern faces. "Okay, okay. How about this one: What happens when Topaz uses her light too much? She gets burned out! Get it? Like a torch burns out." He laughed again, and this time some of the other dragons laughed too.

"Aquamarine, you say the silliest jokes," Emerald said. "That gives me a great idea.

After Topaz has turned out her light, let's start a bonfire and tell scary stories in the dark!"

"Yes!" Ruby jumped up and down. "I love scary stories."

"Me too," said Aquamarine. "Do you know what a ghost's favorite food is? Ice scream! Get it? Like ice cream."

Ruby and Emerald laughed harder this time. Topaz had to admit that this joke was pretty funny, but she could only laugh a little. She did not like the idea of sitting in the dark telling scary stories at all. The darkness was scary enough! She didn't need scary stories to make it worse.

But she didn't want the other dragons to know she was afraid. What would they think of her then?

"We could go back to Sparkle Cave and tell stories there," Topaz said. Even at night, Sparkle Cave was lit up with torches. She wouldn't be scared telling stories there, and even if she was, she could pretend to be tired and go back to her bedcave. She liked this idea much better.

"It'll be more fun out here in the dark with a fire," Emerald said. He settled on the ground and motioned for Ruby, Aquamarine, and Topaz to sit down too. Telling scary stories was a sitting kind of activity.

Topaz glanced at the path to Sparkle Cave. She could make an excuse and go home, like say she was tired or hungry. Then she could leave the darkness and the scary stories behind and no one would know she was scared.

But she didn't like walking around Gemstone Valley by herself when it was dark. Even if she turned her gemstone light on, it would only light up the path, and the darkness beyond could still be filled with monsters. She knew all too well how scary the darkness could be. One time she had been caught in the Friendly Forest during a blizzard in the dark, and that had been very scary indeed.

If Ruby went with her, Topaz wouldn't be as scared. Topaz was sure Ruby would go if she asked. But Ruby was already sprawled out on the ground next to Emerald and Aquamarine, excited to hear the stories. She had even used her gemstone power over fire to balance a fireball between them. Ruby was so brave. Topaz didn't want Ruby to know she was scared.

There was no other choice. Topaz had to turn off her light and stay.

"Okay," she said, as her light slowly went away. "This is going to be fun." But she didn't believe that for one second.

Aquamarine told a story first, and luckily, it wasn't too scary. Topaz actually thought it was pretty funny. It was about a bunny with fangs, but the only things it killed were carrots. Listening to the story, Topaz forgot all about the dark. She laughed along with Emerald and Ruby.

Next, Ruby told a story about a skeleton that grew out of the ground. That sounded very scary to Topaz! But Ruby's skeleton just liked to dance. Topaz was relieved.

When Ruby finished, Emerald gave them a toothy grin. "I've got a good story for you." He leaned closer to the fireball, so the flames sent shadows over his face. He looked scary. Topaz leaned farther away.

"Once there was a dragon who was warned to stay away from the woods." Emerald pointed to the Friendly Forest.

Topaz glanced over and cringed. The Friendly Forest was beautiful during the day, but it didn't look friendly in the dark. "Strange noises had been coming out of the forest, and when dragons went in, they never returned," Emerald continued.

Ruby's eyes grew wide. "Why didn't they come home?"

Aquamarine sat up. "Go on, Emerald. Tell us."

Emerald gazed at each of the dragons. "No one knew what was making the strange noises or why the dragons never returned. When this dragon's best friend went missing, he decided he had to save him. Finding as much courage as he could muster, the dragon strode into the forest and followed all the strange noises. As he walked, the noises got louder and louder, until he saw a pile of dragon bones on the ground."

Ruby gasped.

Aquamarine grimaced.

Topaz trembled.

"The dragon looked up," Emerald said, "and saw a huge leaf with sharp teeth around the edges. It was a giant dragon-eating plant, and before the dragon could scream 'NOOO!', the plant gobbled him up!"

All the other dragons stared at Emerald. Finally Aquamarine clapped his paws. "Yay! That's a very spooky story!"

Ruby clapped too. "So scary and fun, Emerald."

"That plant would've had a burning

tummy," said Aquamarine, laughing. "Get it? Because dragons breathe fire?"

Topaz didn't like the story at all. It scared her, and she couldn't understand why it didn't scare the others. They even wanted to hear more! Topaz clapped too because she didn't want them to know she was scared. They might laugh at her and think she wasn't brave. But inside, she hoped the stories would stop.

Ruby sat up and said, "Tell us another scary story."

"Okay." Emerald rubbed his snout as he thought. "There once was a dragon who—"

BANG!

Topaz jumped at the loud noise. The other dragons laughed.

"Looks like the goblins are doing pranks

again. They love to prank each other more than I love to tell jokes!" Aquamarine pointed at a group of goblins emerging from a hole in the ground. In the middle was Hickle, who was covered in mud and giggling about it.

The goblins saw the dragons and ran over. "You dragons missed a brilliant prank," Hickle said. "Sitch and Pud got me good. I had no idea that if I pulled on that root, all the water would rush in and cover me with mud." He bumped elbows with the other goblins, Sitch and Pud. "I don't know how I'll top that one. Let's go tell the others. This one might even get in the Prank Hall of Fame."

Aquamarine, Emerald, and Ruby grinned as the goblins left.

But Topaz was shaking. Ruby nudged her. "That bang didn't scare you, did it?"

Topaz shook her head. "Me? Scared? Of course not." She forced a laugh. "I thought it was funny."

"Okay, good." Ruby smiled. "Tell us the rest of that spooky story, Emerald."

Before Emerald could answer, Aquamarine yawned. "I'm getting tired."

"Me too," Emerald said, stretching his arms wide. "I can finish the story another night."

Ruby looked disappointed, but Topaz was very happy to stop the scary stories. "I'm tired too. How about I turn on my light and we head back to Sparkle Cave?"

"Good idea, Topaz! Thank you," Emerald

said, and Topaz lit up the darkness all the way home.

After she said goodnight to the other dragons, Topaz couldn't wait to get tucked into her bedrock with her light glowing around her. It had seemed like such a long day, and the scary parts had made it even longer. Topaz hated being scared even more than she hated having broccoli on her boron and onion pizza. She got scared about so many things, like loud noises, scary stories, and the dark. Tonight she'd had all three!

Before she crawled into her bedrock, she made her gemstone power as strong as possible so it lit up every inch of her bedcave walls, just like she did every night.

She wanted to make sure no monsters had gotten inside. Luckily, there were no monsters tonight. She breathed a sigh of relief. She was safe. Soon she'd be asleep and then it would be morning again, with the wonderful sun to light everything and keep danger away.

"Thank you, gemstone," she whispered to the topaz on her chest. "I'm so lucky to have you." She thought all the dragons had wonderful powers, but she felt very grateful that hers was over light, so it would always be with her to protect her when it was dark.

Yawning, Topaz climbed onto her bedrock, pulled her blankets around her, and let sleep carry her away, feeling safe and comfortable with her light all around.

chapter two

A MONSTROUS DREAM

"NO!" Topaz woke with a start. A giant plant with pointy teeth had been trying to eat her!

It was dark, but when she scrambled up, she could feel her bedrock beneath her. She sighed. She was safe inside, not outside in the woods with monsters. It had just been a dream.

"But why is it so dark?" she wondered aloud.

Her light had turned off while she was sleeping, and a scary thought slipped into her mind: A monster could have crept in through her bedcave window!

Shaking, Topaz asked her gemstone power to turn on her light, but nothing happened.

"Turn on, power. Light up my bedcave," she said.

But her light still didn't work.

"What's going on? Come on, light."

The sliver of moon had already passed her bedcave window, and the sun hadn't risen yet. The stars were tiny pricks of light scattered across the sky, but they weren't strong enough to light up the room.

It was dark.

Very dark.

And Topaz was scared.

She concentrated harder this time, connecting with her gemstone power. She wished for her light to brighten all around her, but nothing happened. It was like she had hit a cave wall inside her, a hard cave wall that surrounded her gemstone, and she couldn't get through it.

Fear raced through her.

She wished she had Turquoise's gemstone power of special sight. Then she'd be able to see everything, even in the dark. Of course, if her light would come on, she could see fine. Then she'd know if there was a monster in front of her.

She tried again, but her power still didn't work. Topaz didn't understand. She always kept her light on at night. She went to sleep with it on, and her gemstone had lit up easily every other time she'd awoken before the sunrise. What was different now?

Aquamarine's words played in her mind: "What happens when Topaz uses her light too much? She gets burned out! Get it? Like a torch burns out."

He had said it was just a joke. But what if it wasn't? Could her light really burn out if she used it too much?

Panic rose inside Topaz and she wished, Wished, WISHED for her gemstone power to turn on . . . .

Nothing.

She was still in darkness.

And she thought she heard a noise.

She reached over to her bedrock table,

but there were no torches. She didn't keep any in her bedcave. She never needed torches, because she'd always had her own gemstone light—until now.

She breathed some fire, but it just flickered, then died. She wouldn't see for long like that.

Topaz jumped up, her blanket fluttering to the floor. She raced out the door.

The hallway was even darker, with no windows to let in the dim starlight. All the torches had snuffed out during the night.

Topaz's heart pounded as she reached along the wall until she found a torch. She breathed onto it and a small flame stuttered to life. The torch was only a bundle of twigs, and they were short. It wouldn't last long.

"Stay with me," Topaz pleaded to the firelight. Then she dashed down the hall to Ruby's bedcave and knocked on the door.

"Ruby. Ruby? Can I come in?" Topaz knocked again. Ruby must've been sleeping very soundly. Topaz had to knock hard. "Ruby!" She finally heard Ruby's small voice.

"Huh? What is it?"

"Ruby, it's Topaz. Can I come in?"

The door opened and Ruby peered out, blinking at the torchlight. Her scales were ruffled from sleep. "Is everything okay, Topaz?"

Topaz wanted to say, 'No! I had a horrible nightmare and my light won't come on and I'm scared!' Ruby was her best friend, and Topaz thought she might understand. But then Topaz remembered how excited Ruby had been about hearing spooky stories. Ruby was so brave! What if Ruby thought Topaz wasn't brave enough? What if Ruby told all the other dragons and they made fun of her?

So instead of telling her friend the truth, Topaz nodded. "Oh yes. Everything's fine.

There's just . . . something wrong with my bedrock and it's keeping me awake. Can I share yours? I promise I won't snore."

Ruby smiled. "I don't think I'd hear you even if you did. I sleep like a rock. Come on in."

Topaz exhaled. "Thank you, Ruby. I really appreciate it." She put the torch in the holder on Ruby's bedcave wall, then climbed onto Ruby's bedrock.

"Blow out the torch, will you, Topaz?" Ruby mumbled. "I can't sleep with the light on."

"Sure." Topaz didn't want to blow out the torch. It was the only light in the bedcave. She didn't want to be in the dark again.

But at least here she had Ruby by her side.

Topaz blew out the torch, then stared

into the darkness. She hoped there weren't any monsters looming over her, waiting to eat her. Topaz closed her eyes, but her nightmare kept coming back to her. She tried to tell herself that she was safe. There were no monsters in the bedcave.

But how could she be sure when she couldn't see in the dark?

Worse, Topaz worried she really had broken her gemstone power. What if her light never came back?

As Ruby snored, Topaz stayed awake, waiting for the sun to come and save her.

chapter three

MESSY BREAKFAST

* ·✲· * ·✺· * ·✲· *

When Topaz saw the first rays of sun peer into the window of Ruby's bedcave the next morning, she felt relieved. And so tired. She had light all around her, and she finally felt like she could sleep. Her eyes dipped closed and—

"Topaz! Topaz!" Ruby jumped out of her bedrock. "It's a beautiful morning. Look how blue the sky is!"

Topaz opened one eye. "Huh? Oh yeah."

"We're going to have the best day." Ruby brushed her teeth and mopped her scales.

Topaz rolled over. "I just need a little more sle—"

But Ruby tugged on Topaz's paw. "Come on. We're on breakfast duty with Obsidian and Emerald. We've got to get all the goodies ready before the other dragons wake up. I want to make magma cakes. You?"

Topaz sighed. She'd forgotten about breakfast duty. After staying awake all night worrying about monsters and her gemstone, she just wanted to sleep, but she couldn't let the other dragons down. She slid off Ruby's bedrock and went back to her bedcave to get ready.

Obsidian and Emerald were already

in the kitchen when Ruby and Topaz arrived. They were bustling around, making banana waffles with sulfur syrup (Obsidian's favorite) and cherry calcium muffins (Emerald's favorite). They had even pulled out the ingredients for Ruby and Topaz to make their dishes. Topaz stared at the lumps of zinc she had planned to roll out for her cinnamon zinc rolls. She was so tired, she had trouble remembering the recipe, but she got started anyway.

"This magma is super fresh," Ruby said, mixing it into her cake batter. "I think these are going to be the best magma cakes ever!"

"Is there such a thing as a bad magma cake?" Obsidian asked, laughing. "I don't think so."

As Topaz stirred the zinc into the cinnamon batter, her eyes fluttered closed.

CRASH!

Topaz's eyes snapped open. All the dragons were staring at her. Her cinnamon and zinc batter was splattered all over the floor, and the bowl she'd been using was on her head!

"Topaz!" Ruby ran to her and pulled off the bowl. "What happened?"

"I don't know." Topaz felt her cheeks heat up. She didn't want to tell them she hadn't had much sleep because she had been too scared of the dark. "I was mixing, then suddenly it went everywhere."

"Maybe you were mixing too hard," Obsidian said. "I have that problem all the time."

Emerald groaned. "Only because your gemstone power is strength, Obsidian."

"I can't help it if I'm super strong." Obsidian grinned, flexing his muscles as he helped Topaz clean up the mess.

"I guess I wasn't concentrating," Topaz said. "I'm sorry."

"It's okay. Accidents happen." Obsidian

wiped up the last piece of batter. "Where's your spoon? I don't see it."

All the dragons looked around the kitchen, but none of them could see where Topaz's spoon had gone.

"Turn on your light, Topaz," Ruby said, peering behind a rock table. "Then we'll be able to see better."

"Good idea," Topaz said, but she felt her paws get sweaty. She hadn't tried to turn on her gemstone power since last night. What if it didn't work again? She didn't want the others to find out she was having problems with her power. What would they think?

She inhaled deeply, then tried to connect with her gemstone. *Turn on. Turn on. Turn ON!*, she thought. But nothing was happening. The dragons were going to find out!

Just then, Obsidian came out from the corner of the kitchen. He was holding up her spoon. "Here it is," he said, and Topaz breathed a sigh of relief.

"Thank you, Obsidian." She took the spoon as the others got back to making their breakfast goodies.

Topaz frowned as she washed the spoon, then started mixing her ingredients. Her gemstone power hadn't worked again! What was wrong with her? How was she going to fix it without everyone knowing it was broken?

"When are you going to finish your story, Emerald?" Ruby asked as she got back to making the magma cakes. "I can't wait to hear it. I loved the one about the dragon-eating plant."

"Let's tell stories tonight," said Obsidian, spooning sulfur syrup on top of his waffles. "I want to join in."

"That'll be fun. All spooky stories. They're the best. Right, Topaz?" Ruby waved her spoon in the air.

"Oh, yeah, sure. I love scary stories." Topaz hoped the dragons couldn't tell that she was lying.

She leaned closer to Emerald. "You've got a very good imagination, Emerald. You made up that dragon-eating plant, right?"

"Yeah, I made up the whole thing." Emerald nodded and Topaz immediately felt better.

"Although there are real plants that eat creatures," he added.

Topaz almost knocked her mixing bowl off the table again. "There are?"

"Yeah, but they're really small. And, thankfully, there are none around here." Emerald smirked at her. "Or are there?" He cackled, but Topaz didn't think it was funny at all.

If there were real plants that ate creatures, she had to be able to see around her all the time. She had to get her light back!

Shimmering Hall was starting to fill up with hungry dragons. Ruby breathed on all their goodies until they were cooked, then picked up her magma cakes to take them into the Hall. Emerald followed, then Obsidian picked up his waffles.

Topaz stared at her rolls. They weren't

very symmetrical. She hoped they tasted all right. She hadn't been paying much attention as she made them. She was tired after getting no sleep, but even worse, she was terribly worried about her gemstone. What if she had broken it for good?

"Are you okay, Topaz?" Obsidian asked from the door to the hall.

"Me? Yeah, I'm fine." Topaz tried to give him a smile.

"You look worried," Obsidian said. "If it's about your rolls, don't worry. I know they're going to taste delicious."

"Thanks, Obsidian," Topaz said. She wished fixing her power was going to be that easy.

chapter four

FINDING A FIX

By the time breakfast was over, Topaz was really tired, but she couldn't rest. She *had* to find a way to fix her gemstone power. If she didn't have her light by the time the sun went down, she wouldn't be able to sleep again.

Another thought kept playing in her mind: Could she even be a Gemstone Dragon if she didn't have a gemstone power?

She tried to push the thought away as she slipped out of Shimmering Hall, away from all her dragon friends. She had to do anything she could to get her gemstone power working before anyone found out.

But how?

"I can't ask the dragons in case they discover my problem," Topaz whispered to herself. "If they tell me to turn on my light, everyone will know! So who can I ask?"

She turned and bumped straight into something soft, scaly, and blue. Startled, Topaz jumped back, then realized she'd walked right into Sapphire! Sapphire was the oldest, biggest, and wisest Gemstone Dragon. If anyone had a solution to Topaz's problem, Sapphire would. But Topaz was too scared to let Sapphire know she'd lost her gemstone power.

"Topaz, lovely cinnamon zinc rolls," Sapphire said, rubbing her tummy. "You always put the right amount of salt in. Just the way I like them."

"Thank you, Sapphire. I was afraid they weren't going to be good this morning. I didn't sleep well last night."

"I'm sorry you didn't sleep well. I understand what you mean about being afraid. I'm often afraid about things. Do you know what I like to do when I'm afraid?"

Topaz shook her head, wondering if Sapphire could see that she was afraid about something more than how the rolls had tasted.

"Whenever I'm afraid about something," Sapphire said, "I find I'm much less afraid if I tell myself all the reasons why I should be brave. Like, right now I'm a little afraid I ate too many cinnamon zinc rolls, but I have to be brave because they were too delicious to turn down." She winked at Topaz. "There, I feel better already."

Sapphire smiled, then wandered away down the hall.

"I'm afraid that my gemstone power is broken, and I have to be brave and fix it so I won't be afraid anymore," Topaz mumbled to herself.

She gazed at all her dragon friends still laughing and eating their breakfast in Shimmering Hall. She wished she could be with them without any worries at all.

But she couldn't even ask them for help in case they figured out what had happened. Maybe the other magical creatures in Gemstone Valley would know something that would help her.

Dropping her chin, Topaz walked out of Sparkle Cave and set off into the valley, hoping she'd find a solution.

At the bottom of Mineral Mountain, Topaz found Braidenbeard, the gnome, talking to three fairies.

"Hello, Topaz," the fairies said in unison.

"Good day," said Braidenbeard.

"You look worried," said one of the fairies.

"Nervous," said another.

"Perturbed," said the third.

"I'm all right," Topaz lied, "but I have been thinking about something and maybe you can help."

"Always happy to help," said Braidenbeard. "What's the problem?"

"Problem? Why would there be a problem?" Topaz said, afraid they'd already realized that her power wasn't working. "There's no problem."

Topaz strutted around, trying to show that she didn't have any problems at all, but she tripped on a rock and went sprawling onto the ground. She jumped up quickly. "Still no problem. Why do you ask?"

The gnome looked at the fairies and the fairies looked at the gnome.

"Because you asked for help," they all said at once.

"Oh yeah." Topaz hoped they didn't suspect that anything was really wrong.

She tapped a claw on her snout, pretending that she was thinking. "I was just wondering where all our magic comes from." Maybe if she knew where her gemstone magic came from, she could figure out how to fix it.

"What do you mean?" asked Braidenbeard.

"I mean, for us dragons, our magic is in our gemstones. But how does the magic get in the gemstone?"

The gnome looked at the fairies again. The fairies looked at the gnome. Then they all looked at Topaz.

"That's a very good question," said Braidenbeard. "I suppose the magic is just in there all the time."

"Maybe a fairy puts it in," said one fairy.

"With fairy dust," said another.

"Just a sprinkling," said the third.

Topaz leaned toward them. "Is that really how it happens? With fairy dust?"

All the fairies laughed together. "Don't be silly, Topaz. Fairy dust only works with fairies," they said, then flew away.

Topaz turned to Braidenbeard, whose brow was furrowed as if he were deep in thought. Finally he said, "I've got it!"

Topaz's heart skipped. "Yay! What is it?"

"The magic comes magically!" Braidenbeard stood up taller, smiling big at Topaz.

But she slumped further. Topaz didn't want to appear ungrateful because Braidenbeard seemed very proud of his answer, but it didn't help her at all. She just said, "Oh. Of course it does. Thank you."

She continued to walk, hoping the next creatures she saw would have a solution for her.

Topaz found a group of goblins in a patch of tall daisies. "Hi," she said, but they shooed her away.

"We're hiding!" said the goblin called Sitch.

"From who?" Topaz glanced around, but she couldn't see anyone else. "Because I've got an important question for you."

"For me?" Sitch stepped out from behind the daisies. "I like important things."

"Get back in here." The goblin called Pud reached out from the flower patch and tried to pull Sitch back in. "Our prank will be ruined. Nothing is more important than a prank."

Sitch thought about that, then looked at Topaz. "Ask quickly."

"Oh!" Topaz suddenly felt flustered. She hadn't thought how she'd ask the goblins about the magic, and she had to do it just right, so they didn't find out she was asking about herself. "Well, umm . . ."

"Come on, come on," whispered Pud from behind the daisies.

Sitch looked Pud's way, then turned back to Topaz. "She does have a point. Is your question really important? Because if not, I have a prank to get back to."

Topaz straightened. She had to learn something that would help. "Yes, it's very important. I—" She swallowed. "Have you ever lost your magic? Not that I think anyone has ever lost their magic. I mean, that wouldn't happen. Ever! Of course not. But if it did, what would you do?"

Sitch stared at her, then said, "You call that important? I thought you were going to ask about the best knot to tie when you want a basket to fall on a goblin's head, or how to disguise a hole in the ground so a goblin will fall into it. I can answer those IMPORTANT questions very well. But losing magic?" Sitch started laughing. He laughed so hard the flowers behind him shook. How was that possible? Topaz peered closer and sighed. Sitch wasn't making the flowers shake. The goblins that were still in the patch were laughing too.

Finally Sitch caught his breath enough to talk again. "No magical creature would ever allow themselves to lose their magic. Ever." He shook his head as he stepped back behind the daisies. "Losing magic. Who would've thought of such a thing?"

Topaz dropped her head and walked away. Was Sitch right? Was it her fault that her gemstone had lost its power?

"Topaz, you look so sad." The unifoal Canterlope trotted up to Topaz with his mother. "Are you okay?"

"Hi, Canterlope." Topaz tried to put a smile on her face. "Yes, I'm great. I was just thinking about magic and what we'd do without it. Like, if we lost it, how we'd get it back."

Canterlope's mother shook her head, and a spark of magic sprang from her horn, sending colorful glitter into the sky. "I don't know what I'd do if I didn't have magic," she said. "That's a terrible thought. What if it never came back? What if it left us for good?"

"That's not going to happen, is it, Mom?" Now Canterlope looked sad and scared.

"Of course, that won't happen, Canterlope," his mother said. She turned to Topaz. "I hope you get some happier thoughts in your head." Then the unicorn shuffled Canterlope away.

Topaz sighed. She was no closer to finding an answer about how she could fix her magic, and now she felt even worse about losing it.

What if it didn't come back, like Canterlope's mother had said?

What if she'd allowed her magic to get lost, like Sitch had said?

What if even fairy dust wouldn't help, like the fairies had said?

Topaz hoped none of these were true.

chapter five

NO HELP FOR TOPAZ

Topaz ambled to the bridge over Crystal River and stared into the water. Fish flitted back and forth beneath the surface, as if they didn't have a care in the world. Topaz wished she were like them. She stared at the sunrays bouncing on the ripples. Then she heard a sniffle. And another. And another.

Someone was crying.

Topaz followed the noise and found a goblin sitting on the edge of the bridge, his feet dangling over the side. It was Hickle, the same goblin who had been covered in mud when the dragons were telling stories the night before.

"Hickle, what's wrong?"

"Topaz," Hickle snuffled, "I don't know what to do."

Topaz sat on the bridge next to the goblin. Did he have the same problem that she did? "About what?"

Hickle hung his head. "The other goblins pulled a brilliant prank on me last night. You saw us. It was glorious. Near perfect, although I would've done some things differently, but it was good. Really, really very good."

"Ummm . . . I'm sorry?"

"No, it's a big honor." Hickle sat up straighter. "Goblins only prank goblins they think will do an equally grand prank back. To have such a stellar prank pulled on me, oh, it means so much." His eyes gleamed.

"Then that's wonderful," Topaz said. "So why are you upset?"

Hickle slumped over again. He mumbled something that Topaz couldn't hear. She leaned closer. "What was that?"

"I . . ." He mumbled some more.

"I'm sorry, Hickle. I can't hear you."

"I CAN'T DO A GOOD PRANK!" Hickle shouted, and then started sobbing again. "My pranks have never turned out as good as that one. The other goblins are

expecting something truly epic from me now, but I can't do it."

"How do you know if you haven't tried?" Topaz said. "You might surprise yourself."

Hickle shook his head. "I always mess up one little detail. They're going to see that I can't do a good prank. I'm terrified that they'll find out I'm really just a big failure."

Topaz put her arm around him. "The other goblins don't think you're a failure. They wouldn't have pranked you if they didn't believe in you, right?"

Hickle pulled a handkerchief out of his pocket and blew his nose loudly. "I suppose. But now they're going to find out they were wrong!"

"You don't know that," Topaz said gently. "Your prank might be just as amazing or even more amazing than theirs. But it doesn't matter either way, because all the goblins love you no matter what kind of pranks you pull. You have lots of wonderful qualities."

"They do say I make the most delicious mud pies. I get my mud from right here by the bridge. I find that it's the freshest. Something about the algae. In fact, I might be the best at finding the freshest mud." Hickle nodded as though he was confirming the fact. "And some say I'm the best at having a prank pulled on me too."

Topaz wasn't sure how someone would be good at having a prank pulled on them, but she said, *"Mmmm,"* in agreement anyway.

Hickle gazed up at her. "Thank you. I feel much better now. I can see why all the dragons love you so much."

Topaz's smile faded. Would the other dragons still love her if they found out she'd lost her gemstone power?

Hickle pushed himself up and wiped dirt off his hands. "I've even got an idea for a prank that could be the bestest of the best. I've got some planning to do. I'll see you later, Topaz. Thank you again!" He ran off, leaving Topaz on top of the bridge by herself, wishing she had an idea of how to fix her problem too.

chapter six

ANOTHER SLEEPLESS NIGHT

By the time the sun said goodbye, Topaz's light still wasn't working. She had tried wishing as hard as she could. She had tried warming her gemstone with her paws. She had even tried talking to her gemstone.

"Please, pretty topaz, *please* give me the light again."

But every time, she had been scared

that her gemstone power still wouldn't work, and every time, she had been right.

Now night had fallen and there was no moon at all. Even worse, clouds covered the stars, making Gemstone Valley the darkest she had ever seen it. Topaz needed her light more than ever.

And she was terrified it was gone for good.

Topaz stayed close to Ruby all through dinner and was very happy when Ruby said she was too tired for stories. Topaz definitely didn't want to hear about any more dragon-eating monsters. She was still scared of Emerald's giant plant!

"I forgot to get Amber to fix my bedrock," Topaz told Ruby as they headed to their bedcaves. "Could we have a sleepover in your bedcave again?" She hated to lie, but she couldn't sleep by herself in her dark bedcave without her light.

"Of course!" Ruby gave Topaz a hug. "A sleepover will be fun."

Topaz snuggled under Ruby's blanket, happy to have her friend by her side. Ruby kept her up for a while, chatting about all the things she'd done that day. As soon as the torch was put out, though, Ruby drifted off to sleep, and Topaz stared into the darkness.

She was so tired, her eyelids were begging to close. She had barely gotten any sleep the night before.

But the image of the giant dragon-eating plant had grown strong roots in Topaz's mind. Outside the bedcave window, wind whistled through the trees. Topaz felt sure the noise must be the monster plant.

"Please give me light, gemstone. Please give me light," Topaz pleaded quietly, but even though her yellow-brown scales rippled, her gemstone didn't glow.

Uhhhh.

A noise came from outside the window. Topaz peered into the darkness, but she couldn't see anything at all.

"There's nothing out there," she told herself. "You're safe with Ruby. Go to sleep." She closed her eyes.

Uhhhhh.

Topaz's eyes snapped open again. She tried to see outside, but everything was black.

"It's nothing," Topaz whispered, not

really believing it. "Just your imagination."
She snuggled closer to Ruby.

Uhhhhh.

Topaz sat up. She still couldn't see
anything outside, but that noise wasn't
nothing. She was sure of it.

Clop, clop, clop.

Something was moving out there. Something big.

"Ruby." She nudged her best friend's shoulder. "Ruby, wake up."

"I'm tired." Ruby turned over, but didn't open her eyes.

"But Ruby, something's outside."

Ruby opened one eye, looked into the darkness, then rolled over again. "You're imagining it, Topaz. Go back to sleep."

But Topaz couldn't go to sleep. She stared out the window. And she saw more movement.

Swish. Swish. Click.

Topaz sat up. Something was definitely out there. Was it a monster? Was it the plant monster? Was it coming to eat the dragons?

Topaz wished she could see. She tried

again to connect with her gemstone. "Please. Please. Please," she whispered. But no light came.

BANG! CLANG!

Topaz spun around. Those noises hadn't come from outside. They were inside Sparkle Cave. The monsters were coming for the dragons!

Topaz felt around the wall until she found the torch, then breathed out some fire to light it. It wasn't as bright as her gemstone power, and it didn't shine far enough to see much. She missed her light! At least the torch was a little help to see.

"RUBY!" Topaz shook her friend awake. "Ruby, you have to wake up."

"What?" Ruby rubbed her eyes.

"There are monsters in Sparkle Cave.

They want to eat all the dragons!"

"Monsters?" Ruby sat up. "Topaz, that was just a story. You said you weren't scared."

"I— I—" Topaz didn't want to admit she'd been scared of the story, but now there really were monsters—right outside!

BOOM! BOOM! BOOM!

"That was on the door." Ruby's eyes grew as big as full moons. "You're right, Topaz. Monsters are coming to get us!"

chapter seven

MONSTERS
AT THE DOOR

Ruby pulled Topaz into a hug. "What are we going to do?"

"We have to hide. Come on!" Topaz led Ruby behind the bedrock and pushed her down. They huddled together for a few seconds, then Topaz lifted her snout to make sure no monsters had magically made their way through the closed door into the room. They were safe. For now.

But the monster was still outside their door.

"What do you think it looks like?" Ruby asked. "Big ears?"

Topaz nodded. "The biggest."

"Wide hands?"

Topaz nodded again. "The widest."

"Sharp teeth?"

Topaz nodded a third time. "The sharpest."

Ruby shivered. "I don't like monsters," she said.

"Me neither," Topaz said. They shrank against the bedcave wall.

BOOM! BOOM! BOOM!

"Stay quiet," Topaz said. "Maybe it'll go away."

Ruby slapped both her paws over her mouth. Topaz peered over the bedrock.

BOOM!

The door shook.

BOOM!

The door shook harder.

BOOM!

Topaz thought the monsters would break right through. She squeezed her eyes shut, waiting for that moment. Then . . .

"Topaz? Topaz, are you in there?" A voice came from outside the door.

Topaz's eyes flew open again. "That sounded like Emerald."

"Oh no! The monster got him!"

"Ruby? Do you know where Topaz is?" Emerald asked.

Ruby crossed her arms. "Why is he asking about you and not me? Does the monster not want me?"

"Ruby!" Topaz nudged her friend. "That would be a good thing."

"Oh. Right."

"But you're right. Why *is* Emerald asking for me here and not you? It's your bedcave."

BOOM!

"Ruby, are you there?" Emerald called from the door. "We need to find Topaz."

Topaz jumped up. "I think the dragons need my help. Although I can't think why."

Ruby grabbed her friend's paw. "You can't go out there with the monsters."

Topaz knew that Ruby was right. She didn't want to face the monsters at all!

But something in Emerald's voice bothered her. "Emerald doesn't sound too scared, does he? He'd sound more scared if there was a monster eating him, don't you think?"

Ruby thought, then nodded. "Probably."

Topaz tiptoed to the door, Ruby close on her heels. Slowly, Topaz pulled the door open and they peered outside.

Emerald stood in the hallway with Amber. They each carried a torch, which sent shadows over their faces. There were no monsters in sight. "Topaz! I'm so glad we found you," Emerald said.

Ruby pushed past Topaz, glancing around. "Where are the monsters?"

"What monsters?" Amber asked. She looked around as well.

"We thought there were . . ." Ruby didn't finish her sentence. She looked at Topaz.

Topaz shrugged. "I thought the noises could've been something el—"

"We don't have time now," Emerald interrupted. "Something's happened and we need your help."

"Mine?" Topaz pointed at herself. No

one had ever needed her in the middle of the night before.

"Yes," Amber said. "We need your gemstone light. Come on!"

Topaz's heart dropped. They needed her light. But it was broken.

chapter eight

A PROBLEM IN A TREE

Topaz followed Emerald and Amber to the opening of Sparkle Cave. "Where are we going?" Ruby called from behind her.

"Something is stuck in the big tree on the side of Sparkle Cave, but we can't see what it is so we can help," Amber said.

"The big tree near my bedcave window?" Ruby asked. "That must be what's making all the noise!"

As they got near the tree, Topaz could hear the noise again. *Uhhhhh. Uhhhhh. Uhhhhh.*

Fear prickled inside her. It wasn't a noise she knew, and she didn't like it one bit. What could be making it?

"Turn on your light, Topaz," Emerald said, "then we can see what it is."

"Me?" Panic ripped through Topaz. If she tried to use her power now, the dragons would know she had broken her gemstone. They'd laugh at her. They'd make fun of her. Maybe they wouldn't even let her live in Gemstone Valley anymore. She couldn't let that happen.

"Yes," Amber said. "Shine it into the tree."

"I could blow some firelight up there," Ruby said.

"That could burn the tree!" Emerald cried.

"Oh, right." Ruby looked crestfallen, and Amber rested her shorter arm on Ruby's shoulder.

"Thank you for trying to help," Amber said, "but we need Topaz's light. Topaz, shine it up there."

Topaz stepped back. "Um, it's just that . . . see . . . my light isn't too powerful. I don't think it'll reach all the way up there."

"Fly up, then," Emerald said. "We'll all fly close to where the noise is coming from, then you can shine your light and we can see what it is."

Topaz took another step backward. "Umm, my wing has been kinda hurting." She twitched her wing, trying to make

it move strangely. "I must've slept on it weird. My bedrock hasn't felt right for a couple nights. That's why I was in Ruby's room. Right, Ruby?"

But Ruby wasn't listening. She was at the base of the tree peering up into the branches.

UHHHH.

The noise was louder now, and all the dragons gazed up when they heard it.

Emerald frowned. "If that's a creature, it sounds like it's hurt. I'm going up there."

"But what if it's a monster?" Topaz blurted out.

Amber laughed. "There aren't any monsters around here, Topaz."

"Yes, there are," Topaz said. "Emerald said so."

"That was just a made-up story, Topaz. It wasn't real." Emerald stared at her.

"I know, but you said there really are plants that eat things. You told me in the kitchen. Maybe one of them is in the tree."

"Those plants eat insects, not dragons, and there aren't any in Gemstone Valley." Emerald laughed, and Topaz felt silly.

This was exactly why she didn't want anyone to know she was afraid of things. She didn't want any dragon to laugh at her. But how was she supposed to know what was real?

UHHHH!

"It must be a creature of some kind," Emerald said. "I'll fly up and try to see. Shine your light from down here, Topaz. Even if it's not super bright, anything will help."

Emerald spread his wings, but Topaz said, "No! You don't know what's up there!"

"I'll have your light to guide me." Emerald smiled at Topaz.

Topaz wanted to help. She wished she could. But now she was so scared, her heart pounded. The dragons were going to find out her biggest secret. Her terrible, horrible, awful secret. And even worse, she was letting them down.

She squeezed her eyes shut tight, wished on her gemstone as hard as she had ever wished, and hoped for her light to shine bright as the sun.

But she knew before she even opened her eyes. She couldn't make any light.

She looked at the other dragons and cried. "I can't help. My gemstone power is broken."

chapter nine

A MONSTER FOR REAL

Topaz waited for the dragons to laugh at her, or be mad at her, or both. Topaz had always thought that what she was most afraid of was the dark, but now she realized her biggest fear was losing her fellow Gemstone Dragons.

"What do you mean your power is broken?" Amber stared at Topaz.

"I used it too much, and it ran out of

magic. I turn it on every night when I go to sleep because I'm afraid of the dark. But the night you told that scary story, Emerald, I had a horrible nightmare that the plant monster was coming to get me. I tried to turn on my light, but it wouldn't work!" Tears streamed down Topaz's snout.

"I'm sorry my story gave you nightmares, Topaz." Emerald patted her on the shoulder.

"So your wing isn't really hurt?" Amber asked.

Topaz shook her head. "I'm sorry I lied to you. I didn't want you to know I get scared of the dark. And I really didn't want you to know I'd lost my power."

"I don't like that you lied," Amber said, "but mostly, I'm sorry you felt that you had to lie."

Topaz hung her head. "I was scared that I wouldn't be able to be a Gemstone Dragon anymore."

"Oh, Topaz. We love you." Amber hugged Topaz, her shorter arm squeezing tight. "You will always be a Gemstone Dragon. No matter what."

"I will?"

"Of course!" Emerald said. "Just because you're having trouble with your power doesn't mean you're any less of a Gemstone Dragon than the rest of us."

"And you'll always be my best friend," Ruby said, grinning.

Topaz gave them a small smile. Their words made her feel much better, but she still didn't have her gemstone power, and without that, she didn't feel complete. "Thank you. I still miss my light, though. I don't know how to get it back."

Amber thought for a second. "Our powers are a part of us, like our arms or legs. They get more powerful the more we use them. So the fact that you used yours a lot couldn't be the problem."

"Maybe you're not eating enough crystals," Ruby said.

Amber nodded. "Our gemstone powers will weaken if we aren't healthy. But I've seen you at meals, and I really loved the cinnamon zinc rolls you made. You ate some of those, didn't you?"

"Yes, I did," Topaz said. "Then why won't my gemstone light up?"

None of the dragons replied. They all frowned, as though they couldn't think of anything helpful to say. Then Ruby lifted up her paw. "I know! Amber can fix you. Right, Amber? Your gemstone power is to fix unfixable things."

Amber shook her head. "I can only fix things, not creatures, and I can't fix magic." She looked almost as sad as Topaz. "But I know who'll be able to help. Sapphire!"

"That's a great idea, Amber," Emerald said. "You and Ruby go get Sapphire. Topaz and I can keep trying to . . ."

UHHHH.

". . . help that," Emerald said, looking back up at the tree.

"Be careful," Amber said, then raced off toward Sparkle Cave with Ruby.

Emerald and Topaz gazed up at the dark branches.

"Whatever it is, it sounds hurt," Emerald said. "Topaz, keep trying your light. I'll fly up anyway. Maybe I'll be able to see something."

"Are you sure it's safe?" Topaz asked.

"Sure I'm sure." He smiled.

Topaz wasn't sure at all. She wanted to stop Emerald again, but he was too quick. Before she could do anything, he had flown up to the top of the tree and was peering through the leaves.

"I think I see something," he called down. "Can you try your light again?

UHHHHHH.

Topaz shivered at the noise. She didn't think her power was going to work now, since it hadn't worked for so long. She was scared it was gone for good! And she was scared to even try. But Emerald had asked her to.

Positive that her gemstone wouldn't work, she took a deep breath then tried to turn on her light. Just as she had thought, nothing happened.

"It's not working!" she called up to Emerald.

"You'll get it, Topaz," he shouted back. "I think I see something moving. I'm going to check it out."

"No, wait!" But Emerald ducked behind the thick leaves and disappeared. "Emerald! Emerald!" But he didn't answer.

Topaz was all alone in the dark. She glanced around. She couldn't see any monsters, but that didn't mean they weren't there.

"Don't be scared," Topaz told herself. "Emerald is in the tree, and he's not scared. You'll be fine. There are no monsters here. No monsters at—"

"AAHHHH!" Emerald's voice dove out from the treetop. "Something's got my leg. A monster's got my leg!"

chapter ten

SAVED BY THE LIGHT

"Emerald!"

A monster! Topaz had been right all along. There was a monster in the tree. And now it had Emerald!

Topaz looked toward Sparkle Cave. Amber and Ruby weren't back with Sapphire yet. Topaz had to help Emerald, but how?

She flew up to the top of the tree, but

she couldn't see Emerald or the monster. The leaves were too thick. She was going to have to go inside, but without her light, the thought made her even more scared.

She wished Sapphire were there. Sapphire would know what to do.

Then Topaz remembered what Sapphire had said to her that morning. Sapphire had said that when she was afraid, she thought about why she should be brave. Right now, it was very important for Topaz to be brave because she had to save Emerald from the monster.

"OW!" Emerald cried from inside the tree.

"I have to be brave. I have to be brave," Topaz whispered to herself. Then she pushed her way through the leaves.

Inside, it was even darker than outside. Topaz couldn't see Emerald. She couldn't see the monster. She couldn't see anything.

Her paws were sweaty and she wished she had her gemstone light.

Thinking of what Sapphire had told her, Topaz whispered, "It's okay to be scared, but I can also be brave. I will be brave for my friend."

Suddenly, everything around was illuminated by a warm bright light. It was so bright, Topaz had to squint.

"Wow!" Emerald said. "Topaz, you got your light back. And it's brighter than ever!"

Through the light, Topaz could now see Emerald balancing on a branch just ahead.

"This can't be my light. My light isn't working." But as she said the words, Topaz knew she was wrong. She could feel her gemstone power flowing through her. "It IS my light! It's back!"

"And I'm caught." Emerald looked down at his back leg. His paw was wrapped tightly in some kind of vine.

"Is that the plant monster?"

"I don't know." Emerald's voice shook. Topaz realized he was scared now too!

"What if I was wrong?" he moaned. "What if they are around here and they do get big and eat dragons? Can you see where it is?"

Topaz's gemstone light flickered when she thought about the monster, but then she remembered she had to be brave for Emerald and it shined solid again. Her fear had been the problem!

Taking a deep breath, she climbed behind Emerald and followed the vine. Her heart sped up as she imagined what could be at the end of it. A plant monster? A shadow monster? Some other type of monster?

UHHHH.

The noise was so close now! Topaz gulped. She had to keep going for Emerald. She had to stay brave.

With her light still glowing around her, she scrambled over another branch, then said, "Oh no!"

"WHAT IS IT?" Emerald screamed. He sounded terrified.

But Topaz laughed.

"Topaz?" Emerald said. "Why are you laughing? This isn't funny. Do you see the monster?"

"It's okay, Emerald. I'm not laughing at you. I know what it's like to be scared. But this isn't a monster at all." Topaz tugged on the vines, loosening them from around the branches and then from around Emerald's paw. He rubbed it, grateful to be free.

"Look," Topaz said.

She showed Emerald a clump of tangled vines. Inside was the goblin Hickle. He was fast asleep and snoring loudly!

"Hickle," said Emerald, and he laughed too. "But what's he doing up here?"

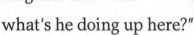

Topaz remembered what Hickle had told her on the bridge. "I've got an idea." She climbed over to Hickle and nudged him awake.

"Hickle. Hickle! It's Topaz and Emerald. You're sleeping in a tree."

"Topaz! Emerald." Hickle groaned. "I'm so happy you both found me. I was setting up my greatest prank. I was going to catch the other goblins when they strolled up the mountain to pick the moonless mushrooms that grow at midnight. They're our favorites, so we pick them and immediately have a midnight breakfast to celebrate. But then I got caught in my own vines and couldn't get down. I didn't want the other goblins to find me because it would ruin the prank, so I didn't call for help. They don't know, do they?"

Emerald shook his head. "No."

"Good! They can't know that I messed up again." Hickle's shoulders slumped. "I must be the worst prankster in all of goblin history."

Emerald chuckled. "I don't know about that. Your prank caught me."

"It did?" Hickle's eyes lit up. "That is wonderful news."

"We heard you snoring and I thought you were a monster," Topaz said.

Hickle gasped. "Pretending to be a monster—that is an even better prank! Topaz, you must have some prankster in you too."

Topaz wasn't so sure, but she wanted to help Hickle. She didn't want him to feel helpless the way she had when her light hadn't worked. "I think we can help you get your prank working again."

"You can? Oh, thank you! Thank you." Hickle sighed. "But the goblins must've gone past already."

"It's not midnight yet," Emerald said, peering at the stars through the gaps in the leaves. "But I think it's close. If we're quick, you might be able to catch the goblins with your prank tonight."

"Do you really think so?" Hickle rubbed his hands together. "I can't wait to see their faces."

"We can do it!" Topaz said.

"What's going on?" A voice rose up from the base of the tree. "Hey, Topaz, you got your light back!"

Topaz peeked through the leaves. Amber, Ruby, and Sapphire were standing at the base of the tree looking up at her.

"Yay!" said Ruby.

"I did! I'll tell you all about it later. Right now, we need your help. Could you come up?"

After the dragons had flown up and joined them within the branches, Topaz explained her idea.

"Yay yay yay!" shouted Ruby. "I get to be in a prank."

"Quiet," Topaz said. "We can't alert the other goblins yet."

"Oh, right," Ruby said.

Sapphire chuckled. "I believe enthusiasm

always has a place in every good venture. Come with me, Ruby and Emerald. Let's set the stage."

As Sapphire, Ruby, and Emerald flew back down to the ground, Amber grinned as her light orange scales rippled and her gemstone glowed. Topaz and Hickle watched as the vines untangled themselves, releasing Hickle, then knotted in just the right places. "There," Amber said. "All set."

"Thank you, Amber," Hickle said, rubbing his wrists. "Thank you, everyone. I can't wait for the goblins to come walking by. Oooh, I think I hear them!"

"Come on, Amber. Let's get into place so we can watch!" Topaz and Amber flew high into the night sky, so they could watch but wouldn't be seen.

Amber giggled. "I always thought pranks were mean, but the way the goblins do it is fun."

Topaz nodded. "Yeah, I'd be terrified if a prank was pulled on me. But the goblins know they all love it, so that makes it much better. There they are!"

Topaz pointed to where Sitch, Pud, and another goblin named Uddle were clambering up the side of the mountain.

"They're over here," Sitch said.

"No, they're over there," Pud said.

"You goblins couldn't find a moonless mushroom if it jumped up and spat in your face," said Uddle. Then there was a pause until all the voices burst out laughing. "Spitting mushrooms. That's funny."

"Did I hear you say you're looking

for moonless mushrooms?" Sapphire wandered over to them, following Topaz's plan perfectly.

"Yes, we are," said Pud. "Did you dragons pick them all already?"

"Oh no, they're too bitter for my taste," Sapphire said. "But we've been stargazing, and I know we saw some around here somewhere. Didn't we, Ruby and Emerald?"

"Over there! Over there!" said Ruby, jumping up and down and pointing at the tree.

"Yeah, I'm sure there were some at the base of the tree," Emerald said.

"Jolly jelly!" said Sitch. "Let's get them. Thank you, dragons!"

The goblins hurried under the tree. Then suddenly there was a loud, "*UHHHH! UHHHH! UHHHH!*"

Sitch, Pud, and Uddle screamed. "A tree monster!" They tried to run, but hidden vines along the ground plucked them all up into the leaves.

"EEEEK! EEEEK!" they cried, their legs wriggling in the air.

Hickle's face appeared from within the leaves wearing the most satisfied grin.

"You've been pranked," he told the goblins as he climbed down.

"Hickle, you did it!" Topaz said, flying down with Amber.

Hickle fiddled with one of the vines hanging down the trunk. Pud, Sitch, and Uddle dropped from the tree, covered in leaves and giggling.

"Bestest prank, Hickle!" Sitch said.

"You are a genius!" Pud said.

"Absolutely brilliant!" Uddle said.

They lifted Hickle onto their shoulders and carried him into Gemstone Valley, singing, "Hickle is the prankest! Hickle is the prankest!"

"I'm glad that tree didn't really have a monster in it," Topaz said, staring at the broad leaves.

"Monsters are terribly scary, but so is admitting your weaknesses to friends." Sapphire winked at Topaz. "You've battled both tonight. You are a very brave dragon indeed."

Topaz felt warm from her snout to the tip of her tail.

"But now," Sapphire said, yawning, "with all the excitement gone, I feel my bedrock calling. Ooh, a moonless mushroom." She reached down and plucked one of the mushrooms from the ground. "I do love their bitter taste. How about we take them to the kitchen? We can invite the goblins for a surprise feast in the morning."

"Good idea," Ruby said.

"Agreed," said Amber.

"The goblins will love that," said Topaz, as Emerald nodded. Then the dragons picked all the moonless mushrooms they could find and carried them to the kitchen off Shimmering Hall.

Once the mushrooms were all stored away, the dragons told each other goodnight. Ruby and Topaz walked back to their bedcaves, and Topaz had a thought.

"You didn't look surprised when I said my power was gone."

Ruby smiled. "I knew your bedrock wasn't really the problem."

"You knew all along? Why didn't you say anything?"

"I didn't know exactly what the problem was, but I thought you would tell me if you wanted to." Ruby shrugged. "Either way, I knew you'd fix it somehow."

Topaz looked surprised. "*I* didn't think I could fix it. How did you know?"

"You're my best friend, Topaz. To me, you're always filled with light."

Topaz smiled at Ruby. Now she knew her friends were her biggest power, and no matter how scared she got, she could always be brave for them.

"Thank you, Ruby." She gave Ruby the biggest hug, then said goodnight.

Back inside her bedcave, Topaz curled up on her bedrock with her gemstone light glowing all around her. Then she remembered Sapphire's words again and decided that maybe she could go to sleep alone in the dark after all. She turned it off, but immediately felt scared.

She thought again about Sapphire's words, then told herself, "It's okay to be scared. And it's okay to use my light. Now I also know that I can be brave too." She asked her gemstone to light up again, but this time she made it dimmer.

With her light around her, Topaz fell fast asleep.

SOME FACTS ABOUT TOPAZES!

COLOR: Topaz gems come in many colors, including blue, violet, green, pink, and pink-red, but the yellow-brown stones are the most precious. Topazes are also clear, so you can see through them.

BIRTHSTONE: Yellow topaz is the birthstone for people born in November.

MEANING: Topazes are thought to help people heal and relax, and to promote truthfulness and forgiveness. In the past, some people believed topaz stones could make you invisible!

FUN FACTS: Topaz is one of the hardest gemstones, and only diamond, sapphire, and ruby are harder. Topaz is also pleochroic, meaning it will change color slightly when viewed from different angles in the light.

Emerald raced out of Sparkle Cave. He was late! Amber had told all the Gemstone Dragons to go to the daisy patch near the Friendly Forest at nine o'clock for a secret meeting about Sapphire's birthday party. Sapphire was the oldest and wisest of all the Gemstone Dragons, and everyone wanted her party to be special. Emerald couldn't wait for the party. He was planning a surprise of his own, and he knew all the dragons would love it.

When he got close to the daisy patch, he skidded to a halt behind Aquamarine, who was looking out to make sure Sapphire didn't come this way. "Has the meeting started?" Emerald asked.

Aquamarine nodded. "Do you know what the dragon who was late to the meeting said?"

"No, what?"

"It was just a matter of time. Get it? Because you're late, you have a lack of time?" Aquamarine laughed.

"Har har," Emerald said. He didn't think the joke was all that funny. He hurried on to the meeting.

When he got to the cluster of dragons,

Amber was asking everyone what they were going to bring to the party.

"I'll bake the cake," Diamond said, grinning. "Sapphire loves my cakes. She should have only the best."

"Okay, Diamond is doing the cake," Amber said, jotting it down in her notebook.

"We'll make the other food," said Topaz, pointing to herself and Ruby.

"Yeah," said Ruby, then added under her breath, "and it'll be just as yummy as the cake."

Emerald tried not to laugh. Diamond always thought what he did was the best.

"I thought we could make a special stage for the party," Obsidian said. "We could act out stories about Sapphire and even sing songs. Do you want to do that with me, Amber?"

"Sure! That's a great idea," Amber said. "What about decorations?"

Opal's paw shot up. "Aquamarine and I can do the decorations."

"Perfect," said Amber. "You're good at that. Your bedcave always looks wonderful."

Opal blushed. "Thank you, Amber. I'm not sure what we'll use to decorate, though. I'd love to decorate with flowers. Sapphire loves flowers! But I haven't seen many in Gemstone Valley."

"I noticed that too," said Garnet. "There are usually lots of flowers blooming around Sapphire's birthday, but not now."

A murmur went through the crowd

of dragons. Emerald could see that they were nodding and agreeing with Opal and Garnet. He stepped back, hoping no one would ask him about it.

"I need honeysuckle for my cake!" Diamond stomped his foot. "Sapphire likes it with lots of sweet honeysuckle."

"I'd love to have pansy petals for a salad," Topaz said.

"Mmmm, yes." Ruby rubbed her tummy thinking about it. "They taste so minty and they look so pretty."

Emerald shrank back even more.

"The stage would look great covered in flowers," said Obsidian. "Sapphire would love that too!"

Opal nodded. "She really would. But where are we going to find enough flowers?

Emerald?" She glanced around. Emerald had stepped so far back, he was no longer in the circle of dragons. "Where did Emerald go? He was just here."

Emerald wanted to hide so no one would ask him about the flowers. He thought about hurrying away, but it was too late. Amber spotted him.

"He's right there. Come and join us, Emerald."

He stepped forward again.

"Hey, Emerald," Opal said, "do you know what happened to all the flowers?"

"Uh, no." Emerald glanced down, trying to avoid the eyes of the other Gemstone Dragons. He felt as though they could see right into him and pluck out his secret. He didn't like keeping secrets, but if he told all the dragons what he was up to, it would ruin everything. He wanted them to be as surprised as Sapphire. He knew they were going to love it. "Maybe they're not growing because of the weather. I'll look into it."

Opal's face broke into a big smile. "Thank you, Emerald! If anyone can grow big beautiful flowers for Sapphire's birthday, it's you."

SAMANTHA M. CLARK is a storyteller, a daydreamer, and the author of a number of books for young readers. Most of the time, she lives in her head with a magical tree, a forest of talking animals, and a sky filled with pink fluffy clouds. Like the Gemstone Dragons, she knows the best power in the world is friendship.

HOLLIE HIBBERT is an illustrator. Like these dragons, Hollie treasures friendships. Her friends help her face scary spiders and remind her to charge her phone. When she isn't drawing or painting, she loves to travel, play the piano, and collect shiny things.

JANELLE ANDERSON is an illustrator who is happiest when bringing the images in her head to life. Some of her favorite things to draw are colorful mountains, sparkly waterfalls, and magical creatures just like the Gemstone Dragons. She loves the outdoors and making people smile, and believes there is a little bit of magic in everyone.